In acquiring a skill, ability grows through daily practice. In learning his mother tongue, the child begins to read only after he is able to speak. The same approach should be followed in music. Music reading should be taught only after the child's musical sensitivity, playing skill, and memory have been sufficiently trained. It must not be forgotten, however, that reading music is taught in order to be able to play without it. Even after they have acquired the ability to read music, the children as a rule play from memory at all lessons.

4. The Educational Method to Develop Ability

When a student gets to the stage where he can play a piece without a mistake in notes or fingering, the time is ripe for cultivating his musicianship. I would say to the child, "Now you are ready. We can start very important work to develop your ability." Then I would proceed to teach a beautiful tone, fine phrasing, and musical sensitivity. The quality of the student's performance depends greatly on the teacher's constant attention to these important musical points.

The following point is very important. When the child can perform piece A satisfactorily and is given a new piece, B, he should not drop A, but practice both A and B at the same time. This procedure should continue as new pieces are added. He should always be reviewing pieces that he knows well in order to develop his ability to a higher degree.

5. Private Lessons

[Parents] and children should always watch private lessons of other children. This is an added motivation. When the child hears music played well by other children, he will want to be able to play as well, and so his desire to practice will increase.

Lessons should vary in length according to the needs of the child. The attention span of the child should be taken into account. If the small child is able to concentrate for only a short time, it is better to shorten the lesson time. At one time the lesson may be only five minutes, at another, thirty minutes.

Shinichi Suzuki
1898–1998

Introduction from the ISA Brass Committee

Suzuki Trumpet School Volume 1 is the first set of repertoire and exercises forming the core material of the Suzuki Method for trumpet. Used by Suzuki-trained trumpet teachers, it is the basis for both technical and musical development within the context of Suzuki pedagogy and philosophy. Foundational work at the "Pre-Twinkle" level should precede this volume at the discretion of a trained Suzuki teacher. Other materials may be used to supplement the technical and musical growth of students throughout their development.

The Trumpet
Instrument and Practice Devices

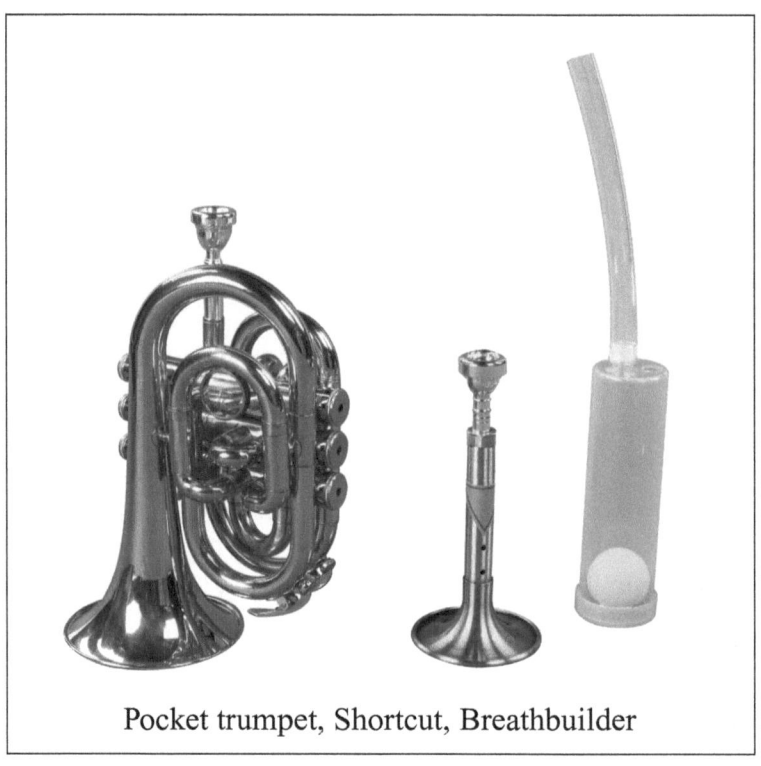

Pocket trumpet, Shortcut, Breathbuilder

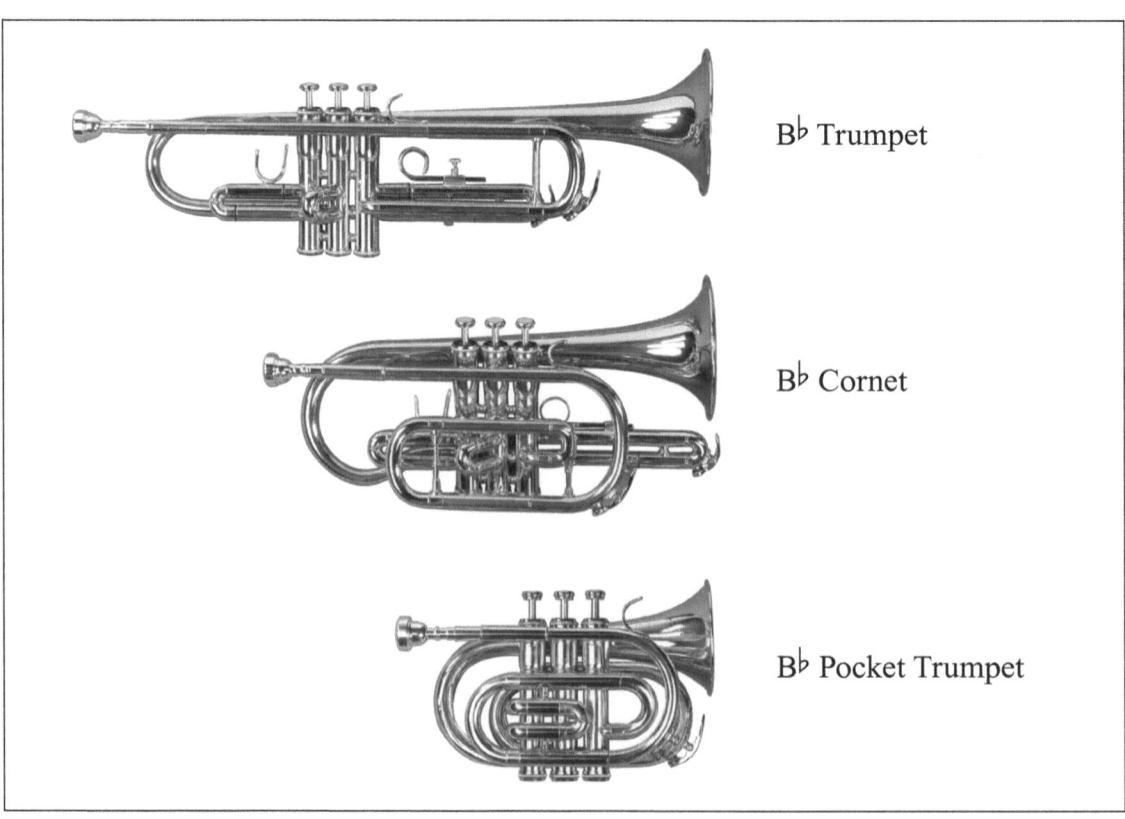

B♭ Trumpet

B♭ Cornet

B♭ Pocket Trumpet

The trumpet is a transposing instrument, meaning that the sounding note is different from the written note. Therefore, when a B♭ trumpet plays a written C, the sound it produces will be a B♭.

TRUMPET PART | VOL. 1

Suzuki®

TRUMPET SCHOOL

Volume 1
Trumpet Part
International Edition

AMPV: 1.00

© Copyright 2021 International Suzuki Association
Sole publisher for the entire world except Japan:
Summy-Birchard, Inc.
Exclusive print rights administered by Alfred Music
All rights reserved   Printed in USA

Available in the following formats: Book (47779), Book & CD Kit (47778), CD (47780)

Book	Book & CD Kit
ISBN-10: 1-4706-4158-5	ISBN-10: 1-4706-4157-7
ISBN-13: 978-1-4706-4158-0	ISBN-13: 978-1-4706-4157-3

The Suzuki name, alone and in combination with "Method" or "Method International", International Suzuki Association, and the Wheel device logos are trademarks (TM) or Registered Trademarks of the International Suzuki Association, used under exclusive license by Alfred Music.

Any duplication, adaptation or arrangement of the compositions
contained in this collection requires the written consent of the Publisher.
No part of this book may be photocopied or reproduced in any way without permission.
Unauthorized uses are an infringement of the U.S. Copyright Act and are punishable by law.

INTRODUCTION

This volume is part of the worldwide Suzuki Method™ of teaching. The companion recording should be used along with each volume.

FOR THE PARENT: Credentials are essential for any Suzuki teacher you choose. We recommend that you ask your teacher for his or her credentials, especially relating to training in the Suzuki Method. The Suzuki Method experience should foster a positive relationship among the teacher, parent and child. Choosing the right teacher is of the utmost importance.

FOR THE TEACHER: To be an effective Suzuki teacher ongoing study and education are essential. Each Regional Suzuki Association provides Teacher Training and Teacher Development for its members. It is strongly recommended that all teachers be members of their regional or country associations.

To obtain more information about your Regional Suzuki Association, contact the International Suzuki Association: www.internationalsuzuki.org

This edition of the Suzuki Trumpet School Volume 1 was made by and is a continuing cooperative effort of the International Suzuki Brass Committee using Dr. Shinichi Suzuki's text and methodology. (2011–2020).

CONTENTS

		Page	Track Numbers*
	Foreword, Suzuki Method	4–5	
	The Trumpet	6–7	
	Preparatory Exercises	8-11	
	First Exercises on the Trumpet	12	
1	Let's Begin, *Traditional*	13	1 41
2	French Tune, *Traditional*	13	2 42
3	Stroll Along, *Traditional*	13	3 43
4	Come and Play, *Traditional*	13	4 44
5	Mary Had a Little Lamb, *Traditional*	14	5 45
6	Twinkle, Twinkle, Little Star, *Folk Song, S. Suzuki*	15	6 46
	Variation A	15	7 47
	Variation B	15	8 48
	Variation C	15	9 49
	Variation D	15	10 50
	Variation E	15	11 51
7	Lightly Row, *Folk Song*	16	12 52
8	Old MacDonald, *Traditional*	16	13 53
9	Go Tell Aunt Rhody, *Folk Song*	17	14 54
10	Are You Sleeping, Brother John?, *Traditional*	17	15 55
11	Long, Long Ago, *T. H. Bayly*	18	16 56
12	May Song, *Folk Song*	18	17 57
13	French Folk Song, *Folk Song*	19	18 58
14	Ode to Joy, *L. v. Beethoven*	19	19 59
15	Amazing Grace, *Traditional*	20	20 60
16	Allegretto, *A. Diabelli*	21	21 61
17	It Jingles So Softly, *W. A. Mozart*	21	22 62
18	Minuet, *J. H. Roman*	22	23 63
19	O Come, Little Children, *Folk Song*	23	24 64
20	Perpetual Motion, *S. Suzuki*	23	25 65
21	Prelude, *M. A. Charpentier*	24	26 66
22	Clog Dance, *Traditional*	24	27 67
23	Song of the Wind, *Folk Song*	25	28 68
24	Allegro, *S. Suzuki*	25	29 69

	Page
Musical Terms and Signs	26
Music Notation Guide	27
Fingering Chart	28

Preparatory Exercises

	Page	Track Numbers*
Tonalization #1	8	
Tonalization #2	9	
Overtones	11	30
The First Five Notes	11	31

First Exercises on the Trumpet

Tonalization #3

	Page	Track Numbers*	
#3, The note C^1	12	32	70
#3, The note D^1	12	33	71
#3, The note E^1	12	34	72
#3, The note F^1	12	35	73
#3, The note G^1	12	36	74
#3, The notes C^1–G^1	12	37	75
#3, The notes C^1–G^1 no repeat	12	38	76

Tonalization #4

	Page	Track Numbers*	
#4A	12	39	75-76
#4B	12	40	75-76

Additional Exercises

	Page
Tonalization #5	14
Tonalization #6	14
Tonalization #7	15
Tonalization #8	17
Tonalization #9	18
Tonalization #10	19
Tonalization #11	20
Tonalization #12	21
Tonalization #13	22
Tonalization #14	24

* Piano accompaniments begin on track 41.

Foreword
Suzuki Method

New and Effective Educational Method

Through the experience I have gained by conducting experiments in teaching young children for more than thirty years, I have come to the definite conclusion that musical ability is not an inborn talent but an ability that can be developed. Any child, properly trained, can develop musical ability just as all children in the world have developed the ability to speak their mother tongue. Children learn the nuances of their mother tongue through repeated listening, and the same process should be followed in the development of an ear for music. Children should listen to the recordings of the music that they are studying or about to study every day. This listening helps them to make rapid progress. The children will begin to try their best to play as well as the performer on the recording. By this method the child will grow into a person with fine musical sense. It is the most important training of musical ability.

Tonalization

The word "tonalization" is a word coined to apply to violin training as an equivalent to vocalization in vocal training. Tonalization has produced wonderful results in violin education. It should be equally effective in all instrumental education. Tonalization is the instruction given to the student as he learns each new piece of music to help him produce a beautiful tone and to use meaningful musical expression. We must train the student to develop a musical ear that is able to recognize a beautiful tone. He must then be taught how to reproduce the beautiful tone and fine musical expression of the artists of the past and present.

Important Hints in Teaching

1. Getting the Student to Enjoy Practicing

What is the best way to get a student to enjoy learning and practicing? This is the principal problem for the teacher and parents—motivating the child properly so that he will enjoy practicing correctly at home. They should discuss this matter together, considering and examining each case in order to help the child enjoy the lessons and practice. Parents and teachers should be sensitive to the feelings of the child. Forcing the child every day saying, "Practice, practice, practice," is the worst method of education and only makes the child hate practicing.

2. Having the Child Listen to the Recordings

If, in addition to daily practice at home, the student listens to the recording of the piece he is learning every day and as often as possible, progress will be rapid. Six days a week of practice and listening at home will be more decisive in determining the child's rate of advancement than one or two lessons a week.

3. Instruction in Reading Music

The student should always play without music at the lessons. This is the most important factor in improving the student's memory. It also speeds up the student's progress. Instruction in music reading should be given according to the student's age and capability. It is very important for the student to learn to read music well, but if the child is forced to read music at the very outset of his study and always practices with music, he will, in performance, feel quite uneasy playing from memory and therefore will not be able to show his full ability.

Parts of the Trumpet

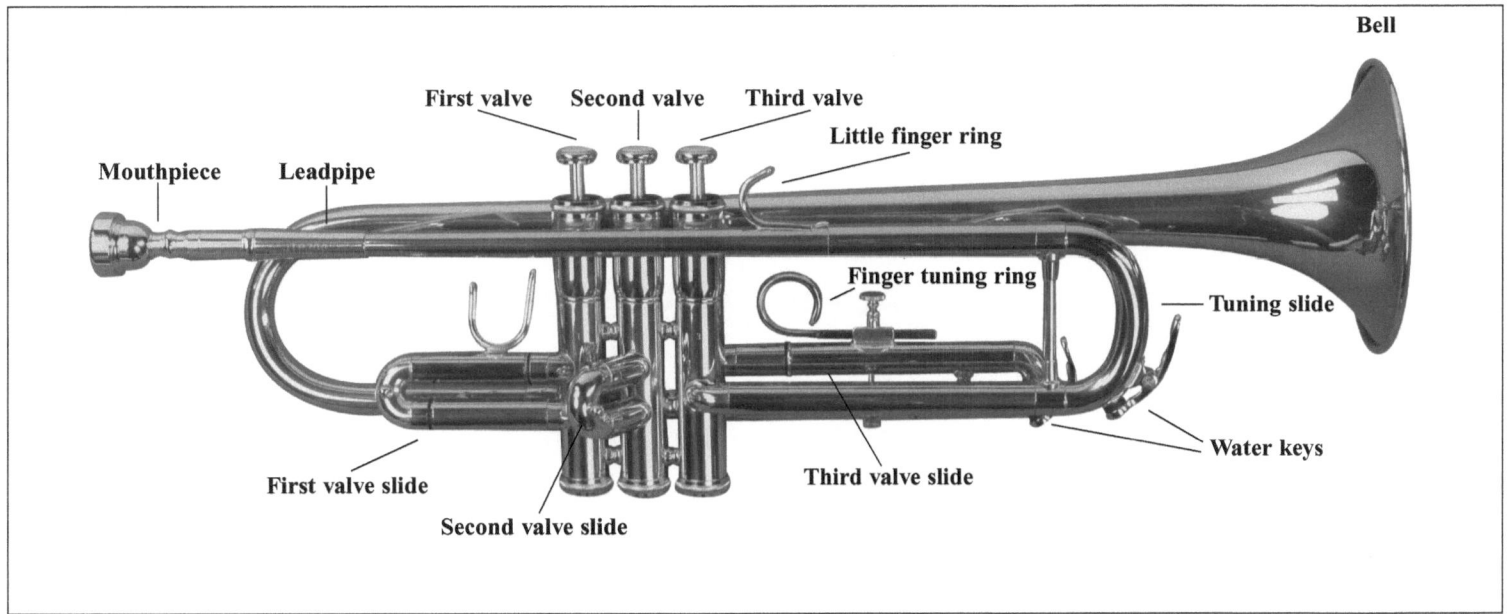

Care of the Instrument

Clean the instrument regularly to avoid damage:
- Clean the instrument as recommened by a teacher or instrument technician. Follow instructions provided by specially designed cleaning kits.
- Make sure to:

    Clean the leadpipe, slides, and valves with specially designed brushes.

    Rinse with clear, lukewarm water.

    Lubricate the valves with valve oil.

    Grease the slides with slide grease.

    Clean the mouthpiece with a mouthpiece brush.

    Dry the exterior of the trumpet with a soft cloth.

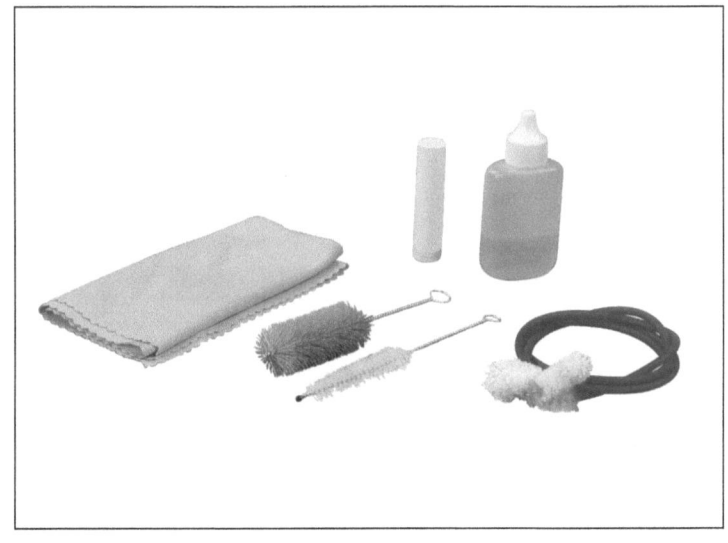

Preparatory Exercises

Tonalization

Use the tonalization exercises in preparation for playing the trumpet. These exercises are essential for the beginner and are examples of exercises that should become part of a regular warm-up routine. The exercises can be used at any point during the practice session in order to establish a beautiful tone, flexibility, and a good articulation.

Tonalization #1
Breathing and Breath Support

Inhale

- Fill the lungs with air as if yawning.
- Put a hand on the tummy/stomach and observe how it expands.

Exhale

- Blow out a steady airstream through the mouth.
- Observe how the muscles around the tummy/stomach help to blow out steadily.

Tonalization #2
Tone Production

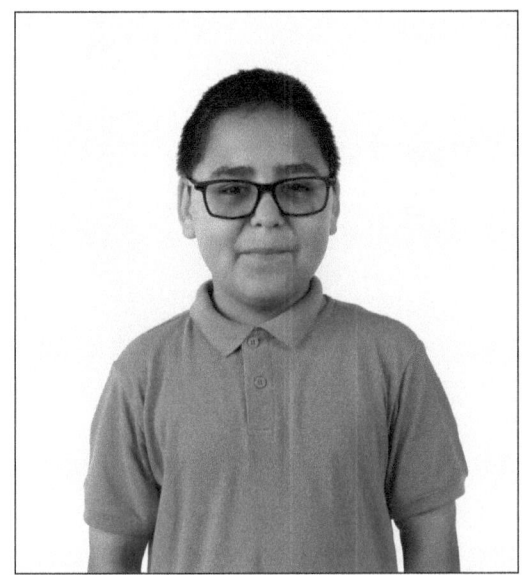 

Lip Buzzing

- Take a deep breath through the mouth.
- Close the mouth and blow a steady stream of air so that the lips start to vibrate.

Mouthpiece Buzzing

- Center the mouthpiece softly against the lips.
- Take a deep breath.
- Blow out a steady stream of air into the mouthpiece to make a buzzing sound.

Play these figures by lip buzzing, and then by using the mouthpiece and/or "shortcut."
Use "breath articulation" (Hu) to start each sound.

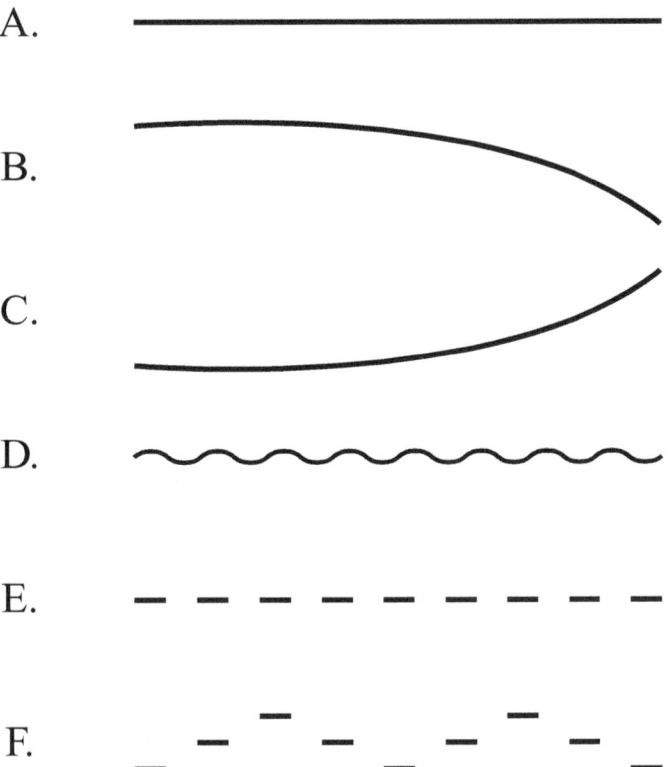

Holding the Instrument

Hold the trumpet in the left hand.

- Hold the trumpet or cornet as if holding a glass of water.

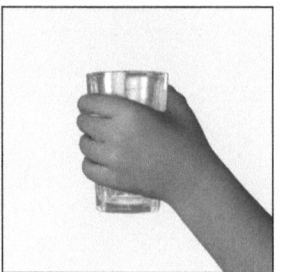

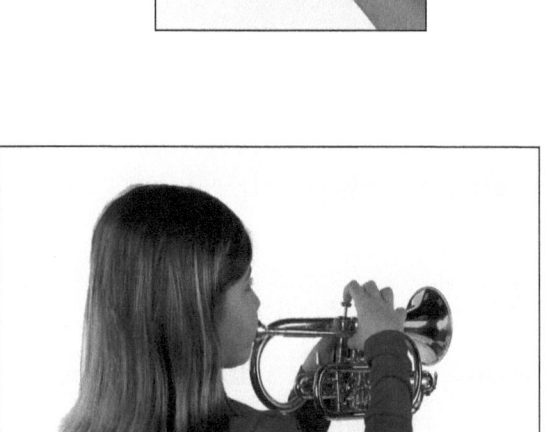

Use the right hand to press the valves.

- Place the thumb under the lead pipe between the 1st and the 2nd valves.
- Bend the fingers softly and let the fingertips rest on the valve buttons.
- Keep the little finger within the natural hand position. It can be placed on top of the hook/ring or loosely inside the hook/ring when needed.
- Consult the teacher for the best way to hold a pocket trumpet.

Posture

Stand with equal weight on both feet and find the balance point of the body. Keep the head up, shoulders relaxed, and arms resting in a natural position slightly away from the body.

When sitting, keep both feet flat on the ground and maintain the same position of the upper body as in standing position.

Overtones

Listen to these three different pitches and learn to recognize them. These three notes can be played on the trumpet without pressing down any valves (0). Refer to the recording (track #30).

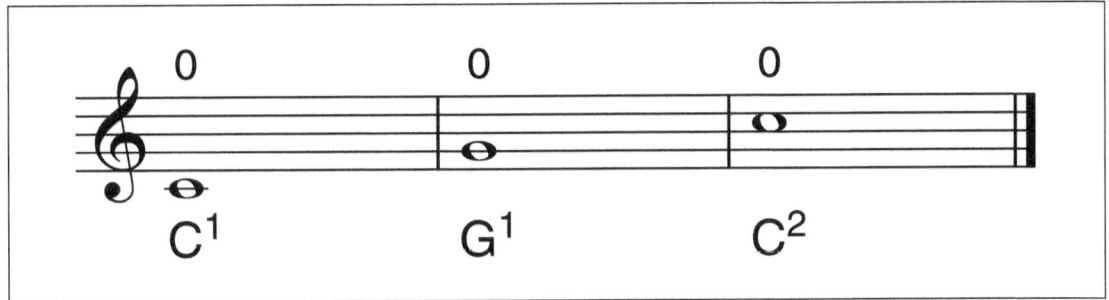

The Valves

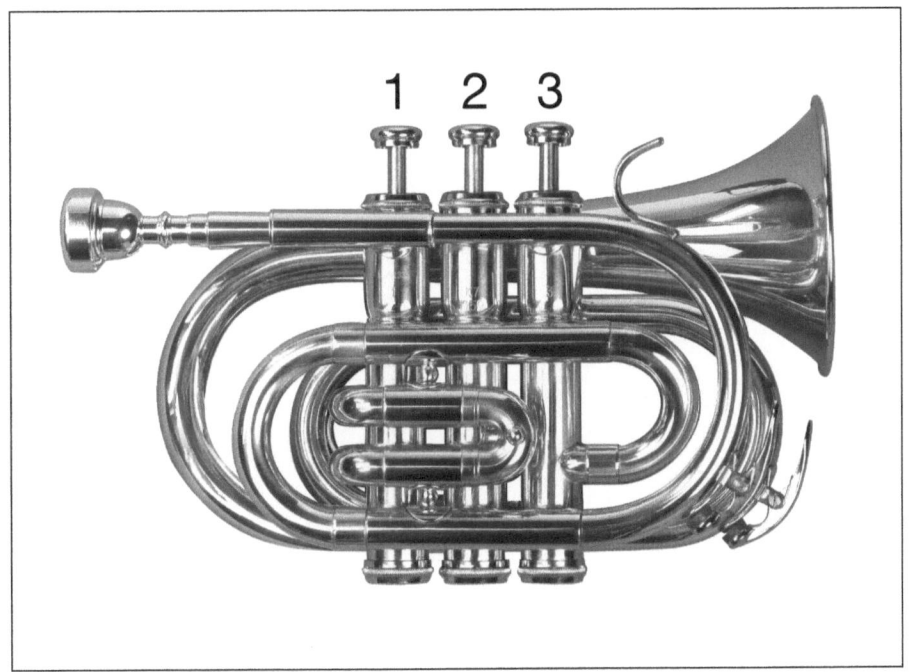

The First Five Notes

Listen to these five pitches. They will be the first five notes to learn on the trumpet. Refer to the recording (track #31).

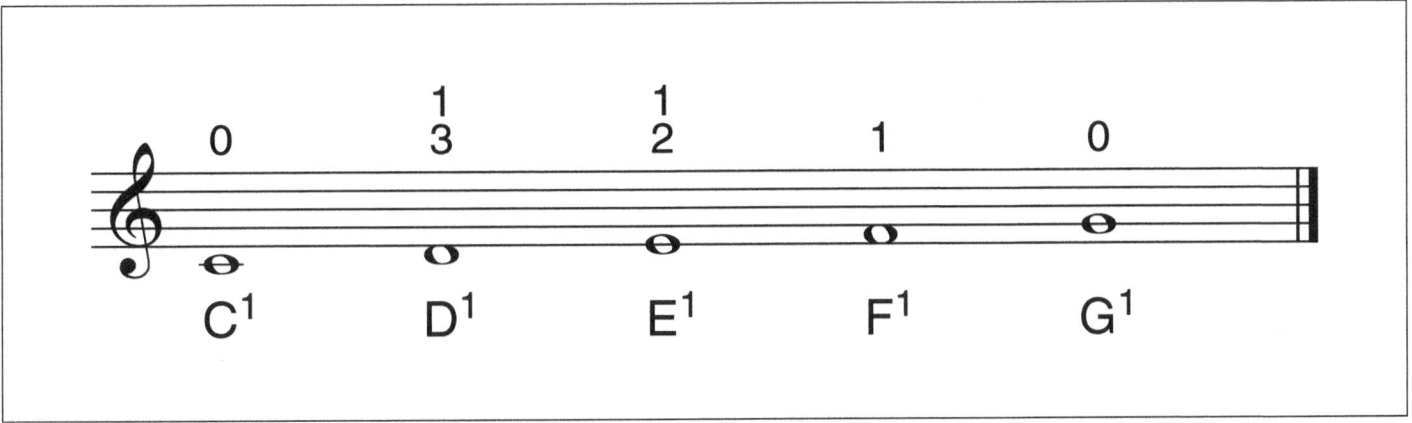

First Exercises on the Trumpet
Tonalization #3
Long Tones

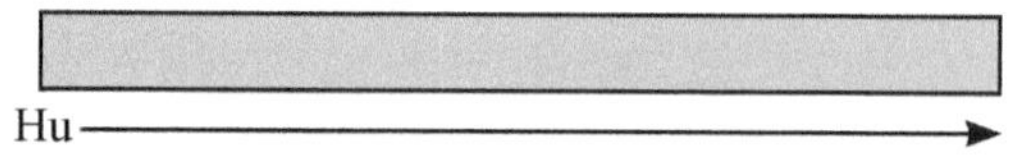

- Start with the note that is most comfortable. Continue to master the other notes in any order.
- Use "breath articulation" (Hu) to start each note.
- Establish a steady beat, inhale in time (over one beat), and blow out in time to play the notes. Refer to the recording (track #32-38). The recording may also be used as play along tracks (tracks #70-76).

The Note C^1

The Note D^1

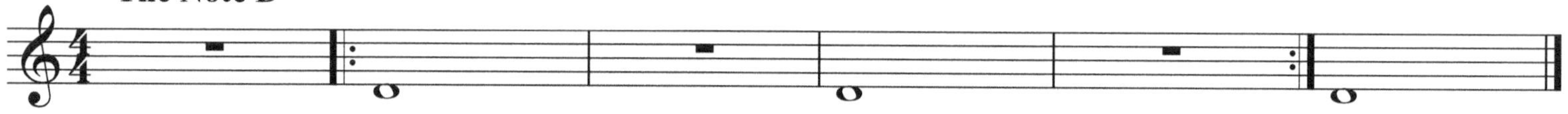

The Note E^1

The Note F^1

The Note G^1

Tonalization #4
Variations to Introduce Tonguing

- Divide the note with the tip of the tongue by pronouncing the sound "Tu." Keep the air flowing throughout.
- Start the exercises with breath articulation (Hu) the first time, then play with a tongued articulation (Tu).
- Refer to the recording (track #39-40). The recording may also be used as play along tracks (tracks #75-76).

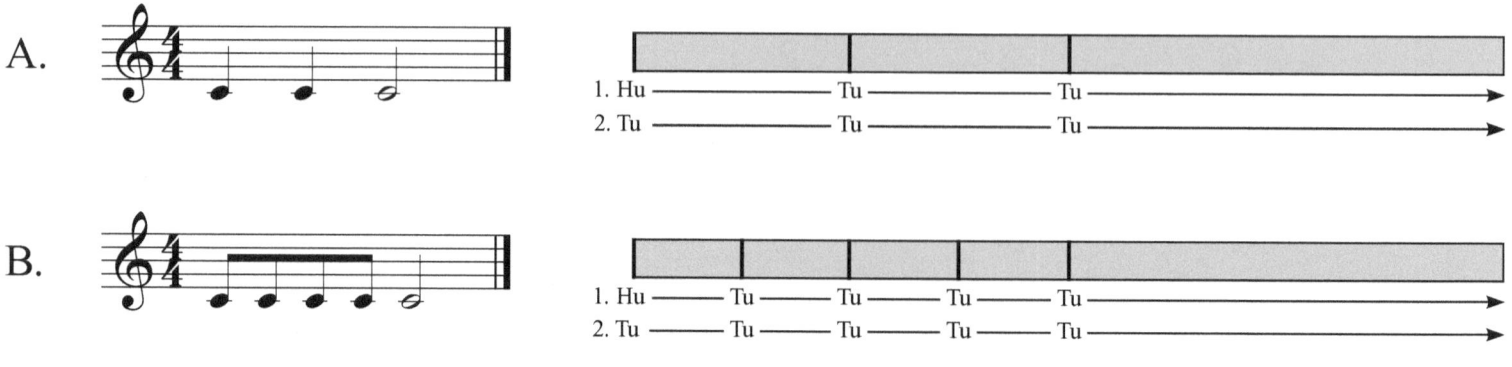

1 Let's Begin

Traditional

2 French Tune

Traditional

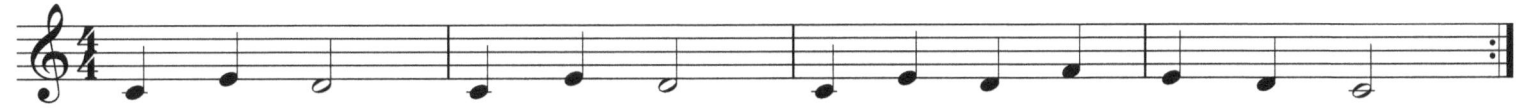

3 Stroll Along

Traditional

4 Come and Play

Traditional

*Repeats are optional

Tonalization #5
C-Major Five Note Scale and Variations

Master playing the scale all slurred first, then apply each variation to the scale.

Variations

A.

B.

C.

D.

E.

F.

5 Mary Had a Little Lamb

Traditional

*Repeat is optional

Tonalization # 6
Long Tone Exercises to Expand the Range

Blow a fast airstream through the instrument and hold each note steady.

The Note A^1

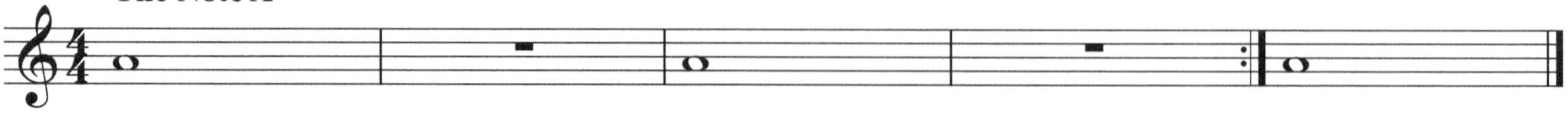

The Note B^1

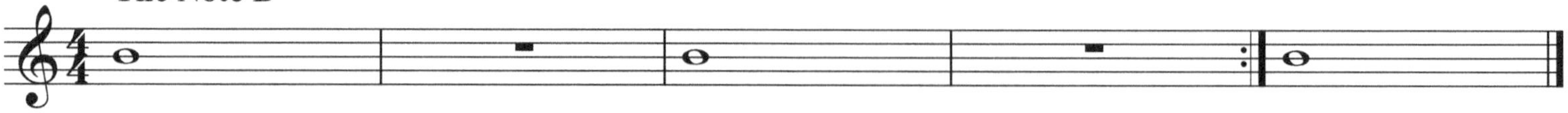

The Note C^2

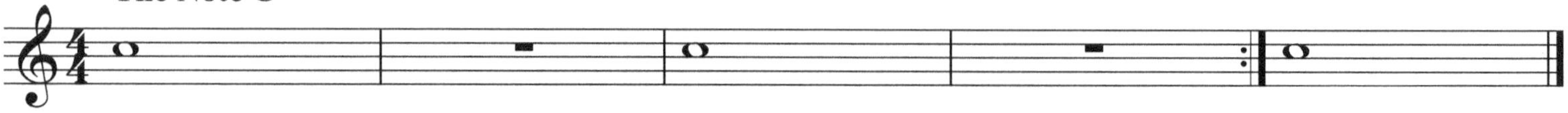

6 Twinkle, Twinkle, Little Star Variations

Folk Song
Arranged by Shinichi Suzuki

Theme

simile

Variations

A.

B.

C.

D.

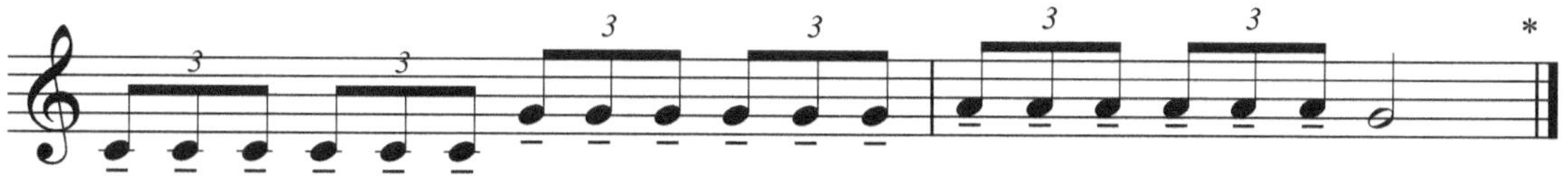

E.

* Variations may be used as optional multiple tonguing exercises

Tonalization #7
C-Major Scale

Continue work on the upper register. Master playing the scale all slurred first, then apply the variations from page 14.

7 Lightly Row

Folk Song

8 Old MacDonald

Traditional

9 Go Tell Aunt Rhody

10 Are You Sleeping, Brother John?

* Repeat is optional

Tonalization #8
D-Major Five Note Scale

Play the scale both slurred and tongued. Play song numbers 1–5 transposed to D Major.

11 Long, Long Ago

T.H. Bayly

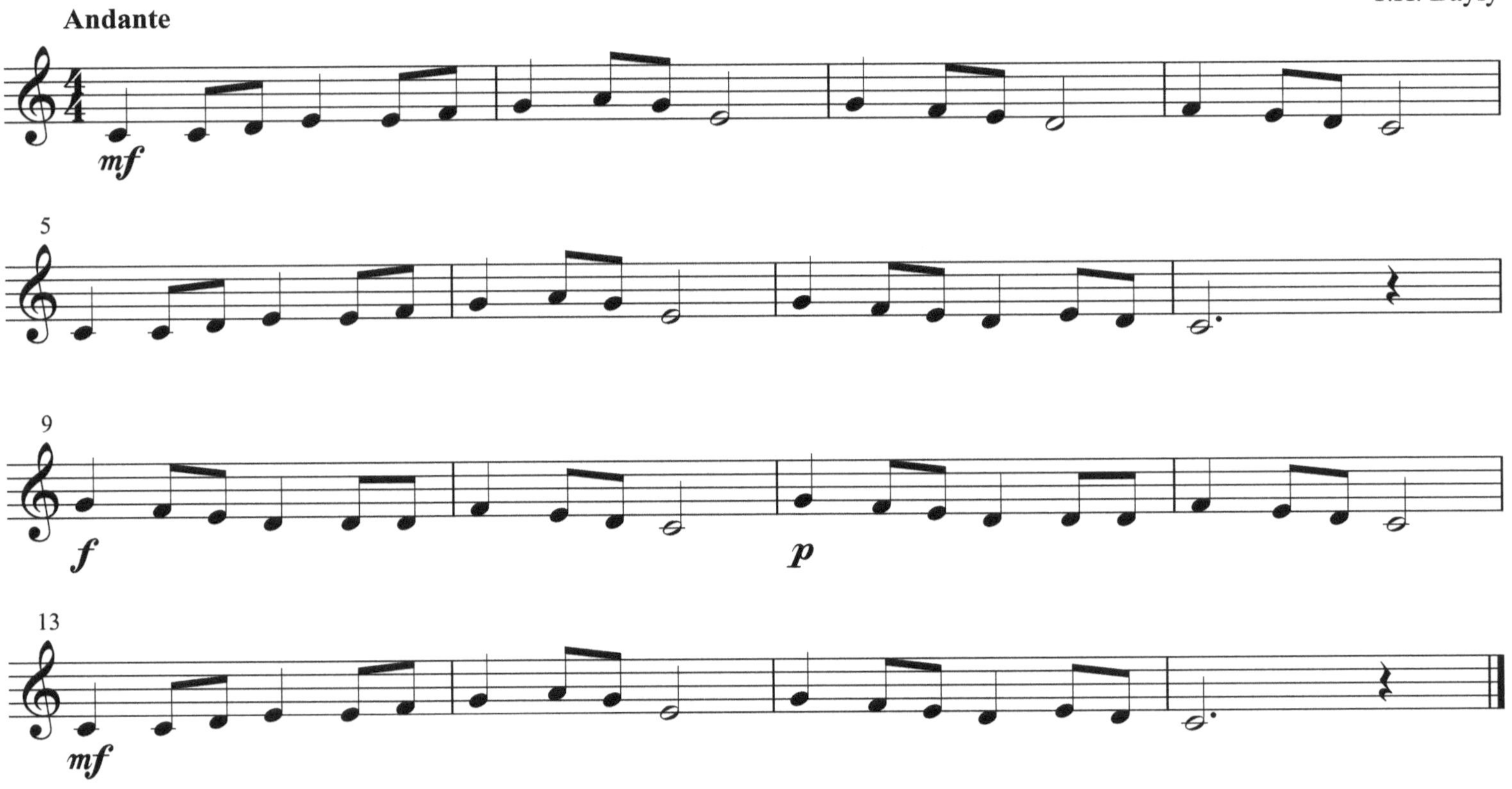
Andante
mf
5
9
f
p
13
mf

12 May Song

Folk Song

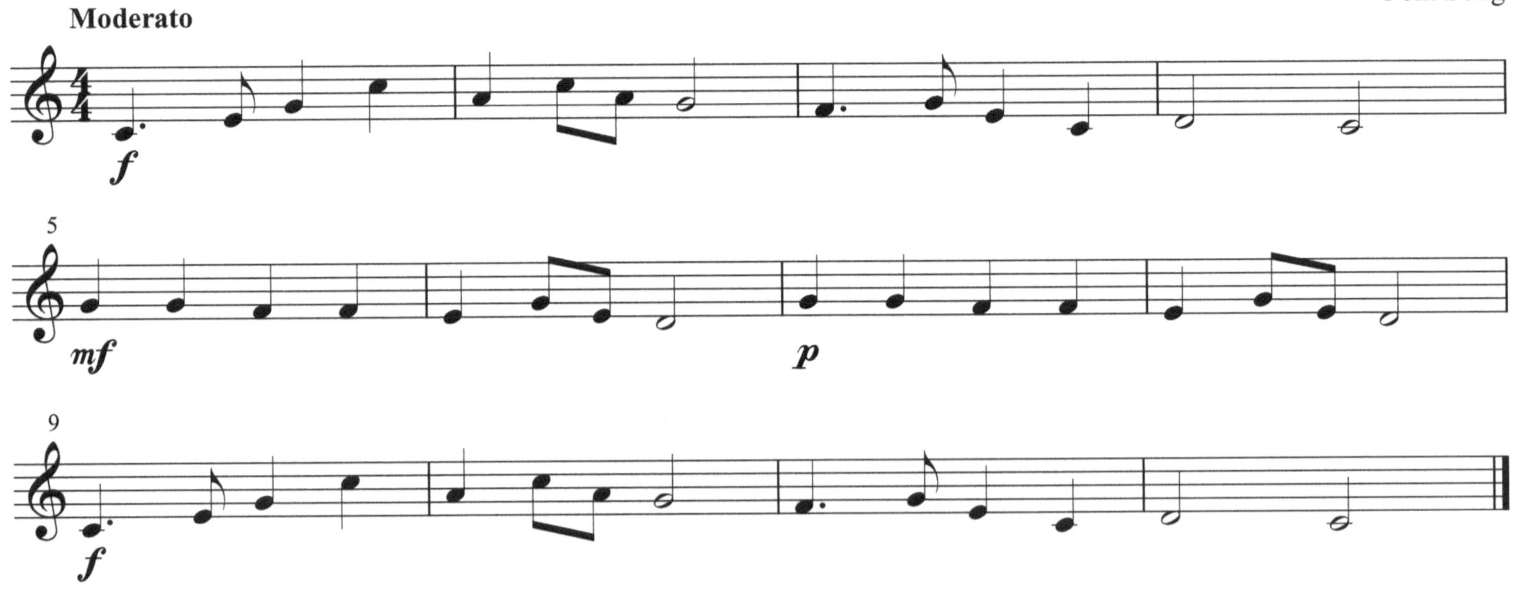
Moderato
f
5
mf
p
9
f

Tonalization #9
Various Rhythmic Patterns in $\frac{3}{4}$ Time

Play the rhythmic variations using the C-Major scale and/or the D-Major five note scale.

A.
B.
C.
D.
E.

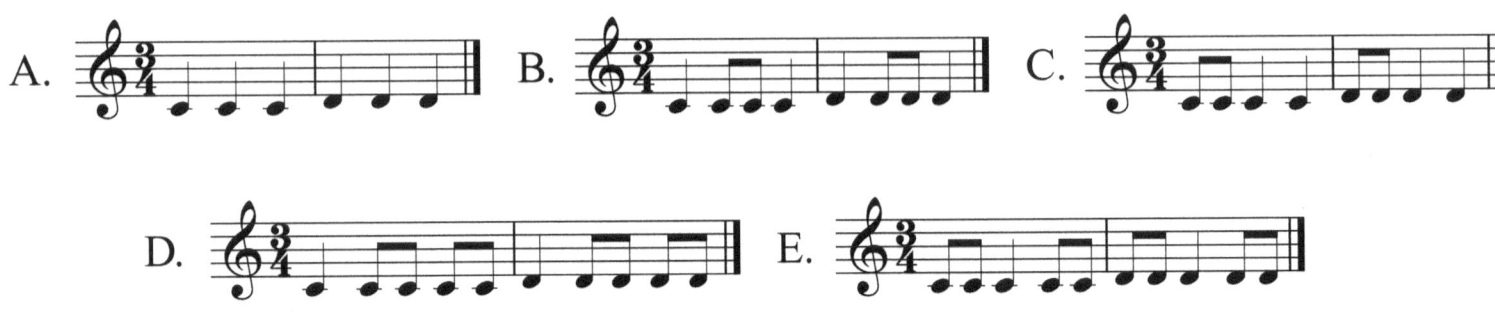

13 French Folk Song

Folk Song

* Breath mark

Tonalization #10
F-Major Five Note Scale

Play the scale both slurred and tongued. Play song numbers 1–5 transposed to F Major.

14 Ode to Joy

Ludwig van Beethoven

Tonalization #11
Lip Slur Exercises for Flexibility

Keep the same fingering throughout each exercise as indicated. Start with breath articulation (Hu) the first time, then start with a tongued articulation (Tu).

*Begin each note with breath articulation.

Variations: Apply these variations to each fingering:

* Repeat is optional

19 O Come, Little Children

* Repeat is optional

20 Perpetual Motion

21 Prelude

from *Te Deum*

Marc-Antoine Charpentier

Allegro moderato

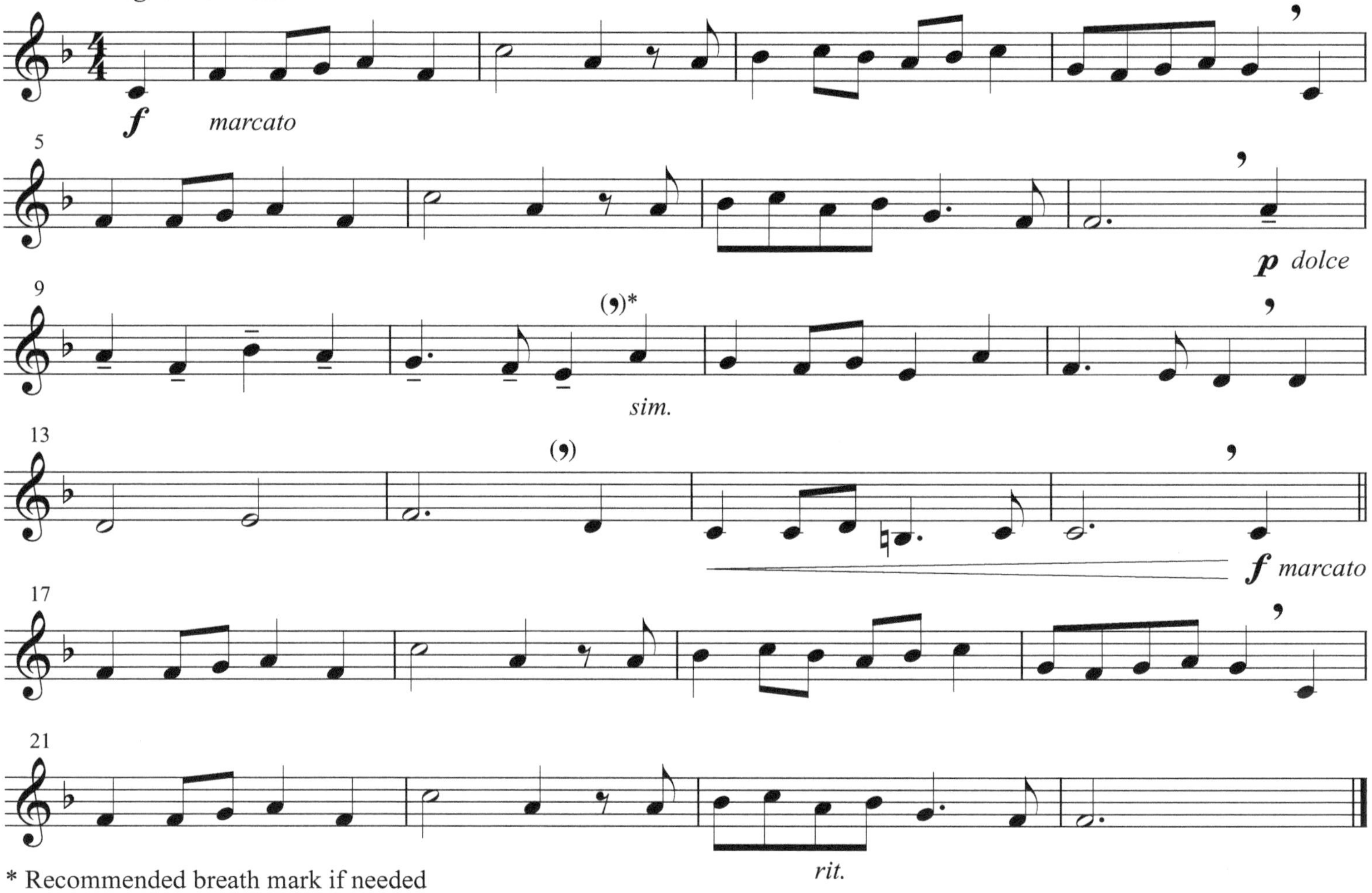

* Recommended breath mark if needed

Tonalization #14
G-Major Five Note Scale

Play the scale both slurred and tongued.

22 Clog Dance

Traditional

Allegretto

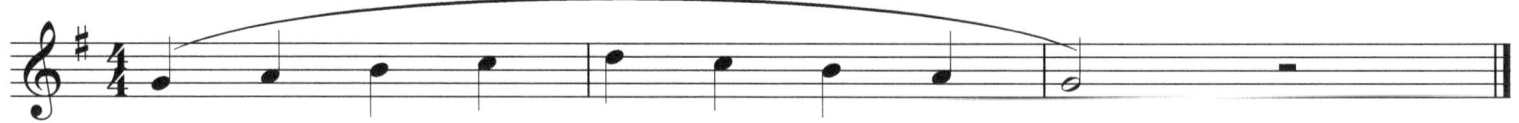

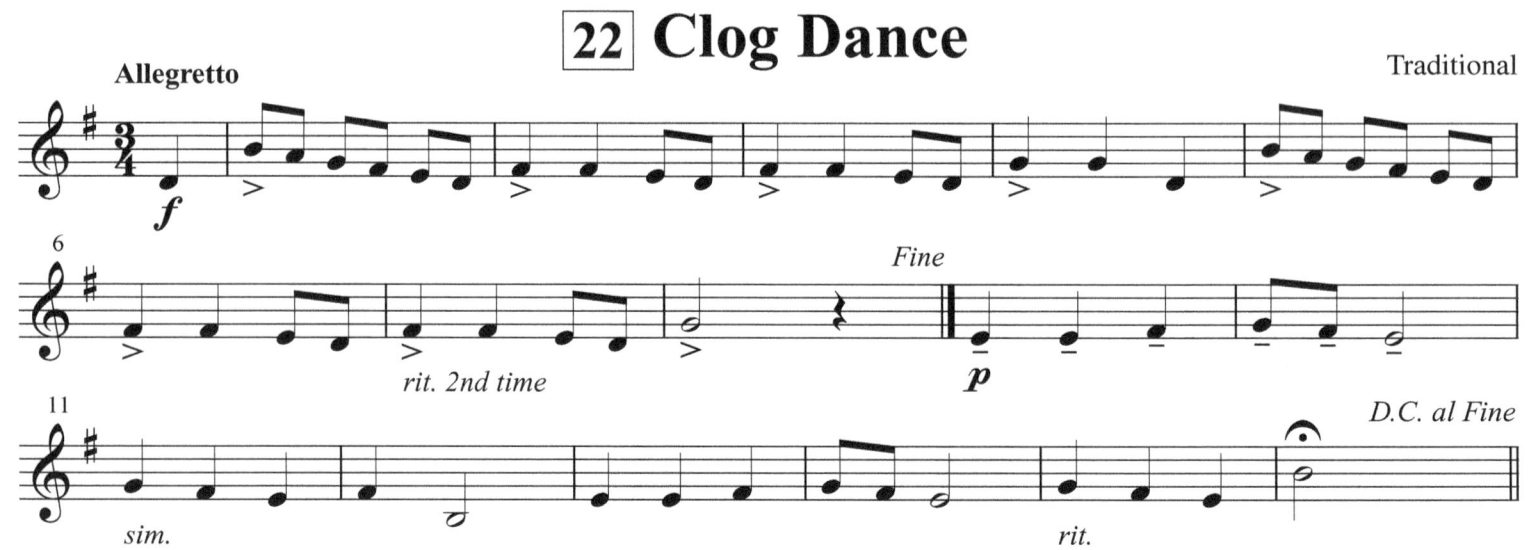

23 Song of the Wind

Folk Song

24 Allegro

Shinichi Suzuki

Musical Terms and Signs in Volume 1
Tempo and Character

A tempo – return to the original speed
Allegretto – moderately quick and lively
Allegro – quick, lively, bright, cheerful
Allegro moderato – moderately quick or lively
Andante – moving along, flowing, at a walking pace
Cantabile – singing style
Da Capo al Fine (D.C. al Fine) – repeat from the beginning and play to the Fine
Dolce – sweet, gentle
Marcato – accented, stressed
Moderato – at a moderate speed
Poco rit. – a little slower
Ritardando (rit.) – held back, slower
Simile (sim.) – continue to perform in the same style

Volume

ff   *(fortissimo)* – very loud
f   *(forte)* – loud
f-p   *(forte-piano)* – play forte the first time and piano the second time
mf   *(mezzo forte)* – moderately loud
mp   *(mezzo piano)* – moderately soft
p   *(piano)* – soft
pp   *(pianissimo)* – very soft
<   *(crescendo or cresc.)* – becoming gradually louder
>   *(diminuendo or dim.)* – becoming gradually softer

Signs

·   *(staccato)* – short, detached
⸱̄   *(portato)* – semi-detached
—   *(tenuto)* – the note is held for its full value
⌢   *(slur)* – smoothly joined. A curved line that joins two or more notes of different pitches.
       (only the first note under the slur is articulated)
𝄐   *(fermata)* – pause, hold the note for longer than its given value
>   *(accent)* – with emphasis
♯   *(sharp)* – raise the pitch a half-step/semitone
♮   *(natural)* – return to the original pitch
♭   *(flat)* – lower the pitch a half-step/semitone
'   *(breath mark)* – indicates where to take a breath
(')   *(optional breath mark)* – indicates where to take an optional breath
⌢   *(tie)* – a curved line that joins two or more notes of the same pitch that last the duration of
       the combined note values.
3   *(triplet)* – three notes played evenly in the time of two notes of the same value

Musical Notation Guide

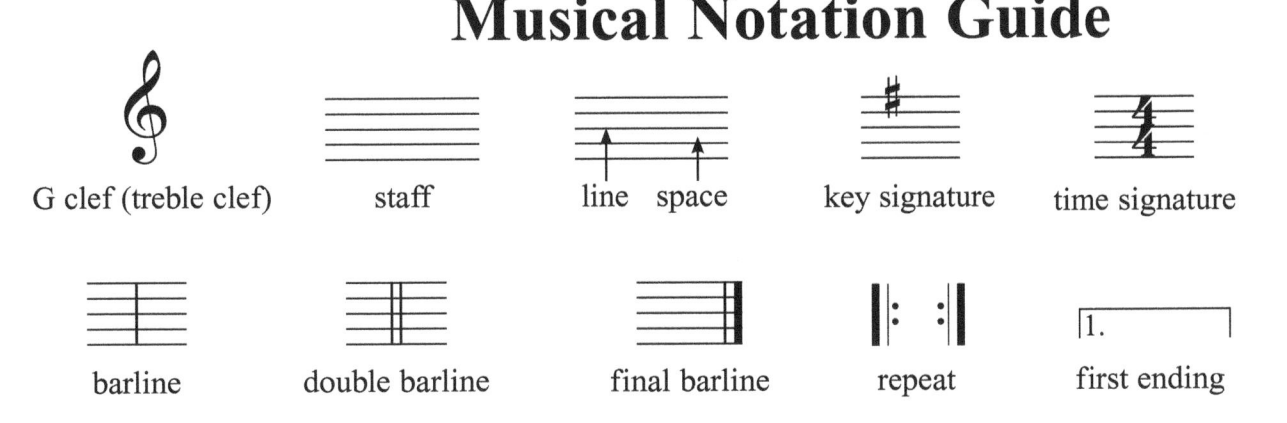

G clef (treble clef)	staff	line space	key signature	time signature	bar or measure
barline	double barline	final barline	repeat	first ending	second ending

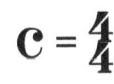 common time

 cut time (alla breve)

---

sixteenth note or semiquaver	sixteenth rest or semiquaver rest	
eighth note or quaver	eighth rest or quaver rest	dotted eighth note or dotted quaver, equivalent to one eighth note plus one sixteenth note
quarter note or crotchet	quarter rest or crotchet rest	dotted quarter note or dotted crotchet, equivalent to one quarter note plus one eighth note
half note or minim	half rest or minim rest	dotted half note or dotted minim, equivalent to three quarter notes
whole note or semibreve	whole rest or semibreve rest or whole bar rest	

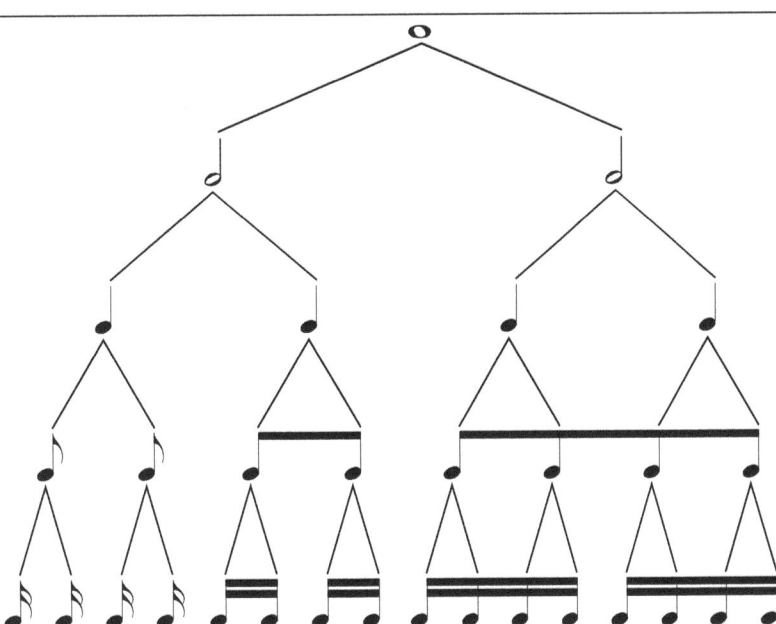

Fingering Chart

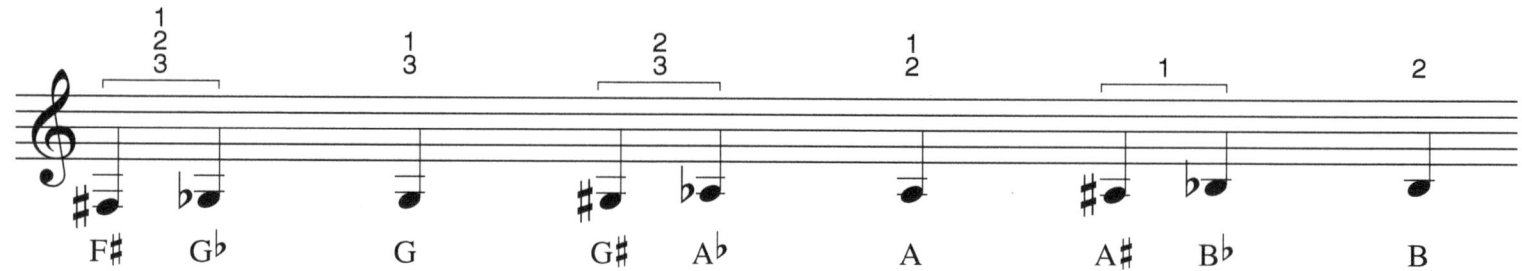
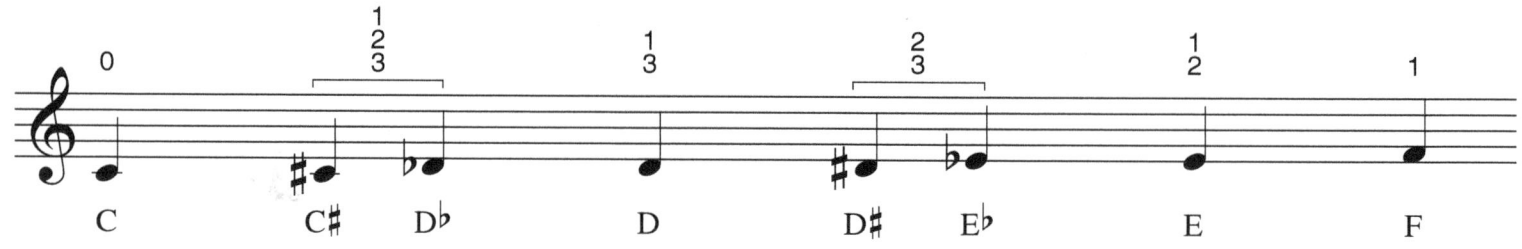
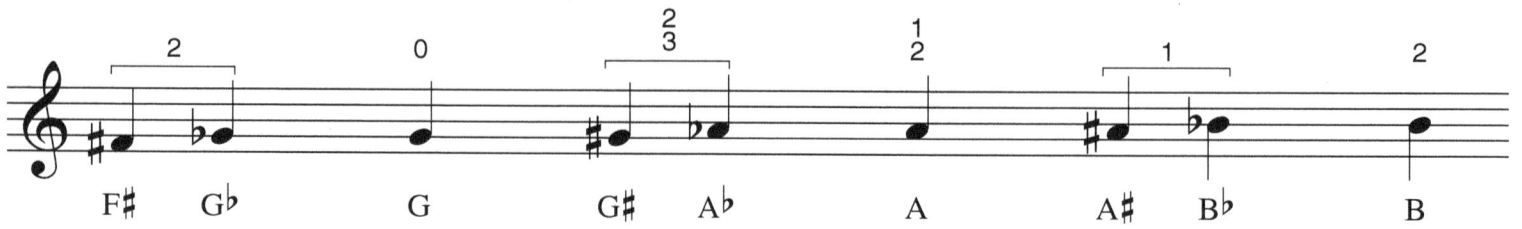

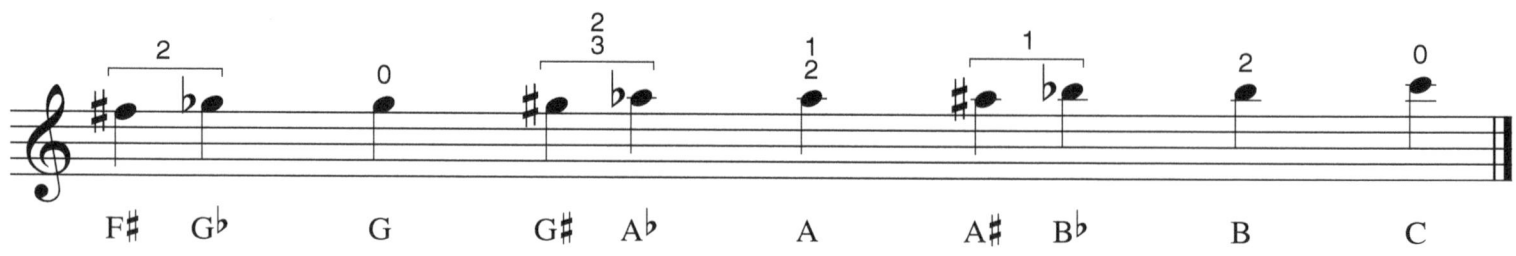